Goat's Coat

Written and  Hambleton

Collins

Goat had a good coat.
It was a red wool coat.
It was soft and snug.

Goat's coat was the best.

Fox had socks.
The socks had pink spots.
Fox did look good.

I wish I had that coat!

But Fox was sad.
Goat's coat was smart.

Fox was mad.
He must get that coat.
Fox plotted to get it.

Goat put up the hood.
She kept the coat snug.
She ran past Fox.

But Fox was fast.
He swung at Goat.
Grab! Rip!

Fox got the coat and ran off.
But the coat was torn.

Goat was sad.
The coat was lost.

Fox felt bad.
He did not like to see Goat sad.
So he got some wool and mended
the coat.

Fox ran back.
He put the coat on Goat.
But Goat spotted Fox's socks.

Goat took the socks.
Fox took the coat.
Fox in a coat and Goat in socks.

A story map

15

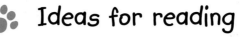

Ideas for reading

Written by Clare Dowdall BA(Ed), MA(Ed)
Lecturer and Primary Literacy Consultant

Learning objectives: read simple words by sounding out and blending the phonemes all through the word from left to right; retell narratives in the correct sequence, drawing on the language patterns of stories; extend their vocabulary, exploring the meanings and sounds of new words; use talk to organise, sequence and clarify thinking, ideas, feelings and events; extend their vocabulary, exploring the meanings and sounds of new words

Curriculum links: Personal, social and emotional development: Making relationships

Focus phonemes: x, oo, oa, or

Fast words: was, the, she, like, to, he,

Word count: 159

Getting started

- Look at the front cover. Discuss who the characters are and what might happen in the story.

- Look at the fast words on a whiteboard. Sound talk each word and add sound lines and sound buttons under each phoneme. Discuss the tricky parts of each word, e.g. *was*, where the *a* sounds different.

- Practise the focus phonemes, particularly *oo* as *look*, and *oa* as *coat*. Write the words and mark the vowel digraphs with a sound line.

- Read the title and blurb together. Notice the phoneme *oa*. Ask children to suggest other *oa* words, e.g. *soak*.

Reading and responding

- Ask the children to read the book from the beginning aloud, using their phonics skills to sound out each word.

- Move around the group, praising blending and accurate sounding out of new and tricky words with long vowel phonemes.

- Encourage children to read fast words fluently, and to reread sentences fluently after sounding out.

- Check that children are following the story by asking them about the events as they read.